The Nutcracker

KAREN KAIN

The Nutcracker

Based on The National Ballet of Canada's production by James Kudelka

Paintings by

RAJKA KUPESIC

TUNDRA BOOKS

Text copyright © 2005 by Tundra Books
Paintings copyright © 2005 by Rajka Kupesic

Special thanks go to Timothy Spain for his assistance with the story.

Published in Canada by Tundra Books,
75 Sherbourne Street, Toronto, Ontario M5A 2P9

Published in the United States by Tundra Books of Northern New York,
P.O. Box 1030, Plattsburgh, New York 12901

Library of Congress Control Number: 2004117241

Library and Archives Canada Cataloguing in Publication

Kain, Karen, 1951-
The Nutcracker : based on the production by
James Kudelka / Karen Kain ; paintings by Rajka Kupesic.

ISBN 0-88776-696-X

1. Nutcracker (Choreographic work)–Juvenile
literature. I. Kupesic, Rajka II. Title.

GV1790.N8K34 2005   792.8'42   C2004-907139-4

We acknowledge the financial support of the Government of Canada through
the Book Publishing Industry Development Program (BPIDP) and that of the
Government of Ontario through the Ontario Media Development Corporation's
Ontario Book Initiative. We further acknowledge the support of the Canada Council
for the Arts and the Ontario Arts Council for our publishing program.

ONTARIO ARTS COUNCIL
CONSEIL DES ARTS DE L'ONTARIO

The paintings for this book were rendered in oils on canvas.

Design: Kong Njo
Costume and set design for this production: Santo Loquasto

ISBN-13: 978-0-88776-696-1
ISBN-10: 0-88776-696-X

Printed in Hong Kong, China

2 3 4 5 6   10 09 08 07 06

This book is dedicated to the dancers of
The National Ballet of Canada,
the students of The National Ballet School,
the musicians, artistic staff - both past and future - and,
of course, to James Kudelka,
whose beautiful production makes magic every holiday season.
– K.K.

To my mother, Eliska,
and to all mothers who take time to introduce
their children to the wonderful world of the arts.
– R.K.

Peter, the stable boy, hummed a tune as he swept the barn floor clean for the dancing to come.

Misha and Marie were bursting with excitement as they watched.

"Can't you hurry, Peter? Everyone will be here soon," said Misha.

"Don't be bossy," Marie scolded.

"Please, children," cried Baba. "It's Christmas Eve. You must stop squabbling." It was no use. Misha and Marie *always* squabbled.

"I can't wait another minute, Baba. I want it to be Christmas," Misha said. "Think of the good things we'll have to eat!" Papa did not like them to eat sweets, but Christmas was different.

"It's the presents that are the best!" Marie hoped she would get a doll, a beautiful doll that looked like a fairy. She hopped from foot to foot in anticipation.

Sleigh bells tinkled in the still air. The children rushed outside to meet their guests.

The guests, dressed in furs and jewel-colored velvets, breathed puffy frost clouds as they greeted one another. Among them stood Uncle Nikolai and his old horse, Eugene.

Now, Uncle Nikolai made everyone who knew him a little nervous. His eyes shone mischievously and he often talked in strange voices. He was the kind of uncle who liked to pull oranges out of people's ears.

"Uncle Nikolai! What have you brought us?" Misha asked the old man.

"Don't be rude," chided Marie, but she joined the others as they gathered around to watch Uncle Nikolai rummage in his sleigh. He handed each child a toy. Eugene gave a frosty snort.

Soon the sleigh was empty. There was a gift for everyone. Except Marie.

Poor Marie struggled to hold back her tears, but she couldn't. She clasped her hands and gave a small stifled sob. In a blink, Uncle Nikolai appeared beside her.

"Why the weeping, my dear?"

She wanted to say, "You had presents for everyone but me!" but Marie was too polite.

Uncle Nikolai drew out his handkerchief. Instead of wiping her tears with it, out of its folds he pulled a doll — a jaunty nutcracker doll with a smart red and white uniform and a helpful smile like Peter's.

"Ah, that's no present! It's too grown-up," said Misha, setting his own gift down.

Marie ignored him. She loved the nutcracker the moment she saw it. She clutched it in her arms.

"Here, let me look at it." Misha grabbed for the doll and Marie pulled it away.

"A tug-of-war in front of the guests?" Papa sounded stern, but he was smiling. The party swirled around them until far too soon, Papa clapped his hands. "Baba, it's the children's bedtime."

The tiled stove made the nursery cozy. Baba kissed them goodnight, but Misha and Marie were restless. They tossed and they argued. Marie felt as if her mattress were stuffed with lumpy potatoes. Misha crept out of his bed and plunked down in a chair. Finally, they fell into a haunted sleep. Mice scritched through their dreams. The old house's night sounds kept them half-awake.

Just as the clock struck twelve a figure appeared in the nursery's gloom. Uncle Nikolai seemed to chase away the fretful dreams and the scurrying mice. He had brought the nutcracker with him and tucked it beneath the spindly nursery Christmas tree.

Marie stirred. "Uncle Nikolai?" she whispered.

There was no answer. The wind sighed in the chimney. Suddenly, the bed lurched and the room began to sway.

A crash shook the room.

"What's happening?" Marie dove under the quilt.

Misha hid his face in a pillow. "I dare you to look," he said.

"No, you look," she said.

"I dared you first."

Bravely, Marie sat up. The noise was coming from the toy cupboard where her stuffed animals sat in neat rows.

As she looked, the door flew open and out poured an army — an army of soldier beasts. Baying hounds and yowling cats clashed across the nursery floor in a terrible battle. They were in danger of trampling the little nutcracker lying half-hidden under the tree.

"The nutcracker! They'll break it. Stop! Stop now!" For once the children forgot their quarrels and acted together. Side by side, Misha and Marie swung at the ferocious toys with their pillows. As suddenly as it began the battle ceased, and the army was once again a soft pile of old toys.

Misha looked at his sister. "If this is a dream, it's a terrible one! I want to wake up."

"Look, Misha. I don't think the dream's over." The little Christmas tree that Baba had placed in a jug to make the nursery festive was growing!

Slowly at first, then faster, its fragrant boughs reached toward the walls. Its tip touched the ceiling. It shuddered and shook, the pretty ornaments banging together like drums of war. Under it, the wooden nutcracker was growing too, until it stood alive before them.

"Misha! He looks like Peter, the stable boy!" Marie was thrilled.

Indeed, the Nutcracker Prince spoke in a kind voice just like Peter's. "You were brave this evening, and you set aside your differences to save me. As a reward I promise you a night of wonders."

With that, the room began to spin once more.

The walls fell away. The glowing stove vanished. The toy cupboard disappeared. The familiar nursery was gone. Misha and Marie found themselves deep in a dark, still forest. Although the air was frigid, they felt no cold. They stood silently hand in hand.

Snowflakes skittered across a frozen lake and icy branches creaked as they moved in the frosty night. A light shimmered, and soft as moonlight, the Snow Queen appeared.

"Welcome to my realm," she said, and dipped in a graceful curtsy. "I'm sending you on a journey."

"Where are we going?" asked Misha.

"To a place you've never dreamed of."

Marie was delighted when a shiplike sleigh drew up, pulled by a white unicorn and driven by a handsome prince. "Oh, Misha, it's the nutcracker," she said.

Misha was amazed. "Where is he taking us?" Marie could hardly believe the wonder of it all.

As the iceboat carried them to a secret kingdom, the gates of the domed palace swung open to greet them.

They were welcomed in by a stately Grand Duke and Duchess. In the center of the great hall stood a large, golden egg swathed in ribbons and jewels. The sides of the egg parted and the children saw that it was lined with sky blue silk studded with stars. Inside was a sparkling figure.

"Who is she?" Marie gasped.

"The Sugar Plum Fairy. This is her palace," declared the Grand Duchess.

Sweet as an angel and light as foam, she danced on the tips of her toes. All the while, the Nutcracker Prince stood at attention smiling at her.

When the dance ended, the Nutcracker Prince told the courtiers about the battle of the cats and dogs. Everyone rose to cheer Misha and Marie.

"Guests of honor, we salute you!" they cried.

"This calls for a banquet," announced the Grand Duke. "In this land we always start our meals with chocolate." He clapped his hands and a great table appeared. Its snowy cloth was covered with sweets.

A chef in a tall white hat appeared. The chocolate cupcakes on the table looked delicious until Marie reached for one and it began to move. She pulled back her hand and watched as tiny Spanish dancers performed a dignified flamenco.

"Will you have cocoa, my dear?" The chef offered a cup to Misha.

Misha was amazed to see delicate figures skimming along on the bubbles. "Oh, no! We aren't allowed. . . ."

"It's all topsy-turvy in this palace," said Marie as she rubbed her eyes.

"I know," said Misha. "I can't find my bearings. Is that Uncle Nikolai or the Grand Duke?"

"I don't know. And is that the Grand Duchess or is it Baba?" asked Marie.

As the children watched and puzzled, the Grand Duchess and a gentle shepherdess did a stately dance while a herd of fluffy sheep gathered about.

The doors of the hall clanged open and chefs brought in more good things to eat. The music and the dancing and the mouth-watering aromas made the children dizzy.

"Everything is different here," said Marie, "but familiar all the same."

"Watch, children, there is one more wonder yet to come," said the Sugar Plum Fairy. With a wave of her wand, the loveliest treat of all appeared.

Blossoms of yellow and blue and white tossed in the fragrant breeze that flowed into the room. The flowers waltzed joyfully and opened their arms to the sun. Sweet music filled the air.

The darkness of winter promised to give way to spring and the whole world would be renewed.

The time had come to leave the palace. Misha offered Marie his arm as they prepared to bid farewell to the Grand Duchess and the Grand Duke, the Sugar Plum Fairy, and the Nutcracker Prince. But before they could speak, the walls of the palace fell away around them. The tables groaning with cakes and chocolate vanished. The courtiers in their silks and satins disappeared. In a wink, the children found themselves back in the nursery as the snow fell silently against the window.

"Are we home?" murmured Misha. "I've had the strangest dream." He snuggled into his pillow.

"So have I," said Marie. With her fingertips she stroked the glossy wood of the nutcracker that now stood guard by her bed. She smiled as she fell into a dreamless sleep.